Contents

Chapter 1
ON THE WAY HOME

Mama Rex and T walked out of the pizza place, into the evening.

On the sidewalk, a man was playing a xylophone. He had a squeezing expression on his face.

Mama Rex and T stopped to listen.

"Nice," said T.

"Yes," said Mama Rex. "But we have to get going."

T nodded. He had forgotten they were in a hurry. Mama Rex had work she had to finish.

MAMA REX AND T
Stay up Late

by Rachel Vail
illustrations by Steve Björkman

SCHOLASTIC INC.
New York Toronto London Auckland Sydney
Mexico City New Delhi Hong Kong

To Fran, Jean, Craig, and Kathryn,
you are exactly what my work needed.
—RV

For Gracie with love
—SB

ISBN 0-439-19921-2

Text copyright © 2001 by Rachel Vail.
Art copyright © 2001 by Steve Björkman.

All rights reserved. Published by Scholastic Inc.
SCHOLASTIC and associated logos are trademarks and/or
registered trademarks of Scholastic Inc.

12 11 10 9 8 7 6 5 4 3   1 2 3 4 5 6 7/0

Book design by Cristina Costantino

Printed in the U.S.A.
First Scholastic printing, March 2001

T held Mama Rex's hand and skipped along to keep up.

Women and men barked into cell phones and swarmed in every direction.

Taxis swerved and honked.

T hopped down off the curb and crossed the street with Mama Rex.

A horse pulled a carriage full of people who weren't Cinderella.

"Do you think that was once a pumpkin?" T asked.

Mama Rex wasn't looking at the carriage. She was looking at her watch.

T ran ahead and went through the revolving
door of their building. He waved at Freddie, the
doorman, and hid under the lobby table. T saw
Mama Rex's legs.

"I lost a young dinosaur," said Mama Rex. "Has
anyone seen a dinosaur?"

T tried to hold in his giggles. It didn't work.
Snorting noises squeezed out.

Mama Rex's legs stopped. "Hmm," she said. "That was a strange noise. But not a dinosaur noise. More like a pig noise. Too bad I'm not looking for a pig."

T clapped his hand over his mouth and pinched his nose shut. A long, loud squeal burst through.

Mama Rex's legs turned around. "Now that sounds like an elephant," she said. "What a shame. An elephant can't help me get the mail."

Mama Rex's legs walked toward the mail room.

T bolted out of his hiding place. He loved getting the mail.

"Boo!" T yelled.

Mama Rex jumped. She dropped her bag of leftover pizza.

"Did I really scare you?" asked T.

"I was scared I'd have to get the mail myself," answered Mama Rex. She handed the key to T.

T reached up and slipped the key into the lock of their mailbox, 15M. He turned it and pulled out a pile of mail.

In the elevator, T sorted through the stack of envelopes. Anything for someone named Resident he got to keep.

"Two!" he said. His record was six, one day last January.

T skipped down the hall.

He was a fast skipper but Mama Rex was an even faster walker. She had very powerful legs, and she was in a hurry.

When they got to their door, Mama Rex held out her hand for the keys.

"I can do it," said T.

Mama Rex tapped her claws against the door while T unlocked it. "I'm sorry to rush," said Mama Rex. "But I have work to finish tonight."

"I know," said T.

T took off his jacket and brought it straight
to his coatrack.

Mama Rex was listening to the answering
machine, kicking off her shoes, rummaging
through her briefcase, and grumbling, all at once.

"I could help you," T offered.

"Oh, T," sighed Mama Rex. "I wish you could.
But what I really need is just to concentrate.
Can you find something quiet to do?"

"Sure I can," said T helpfully.

Chapter 2
Oops!

Mama Rex sat at the table and spread out her papers.

T went into his room and looked for something quiet to do.

He poured out his collection of round rocks. They skittered and clattered noisily across his floor.

"Oops," said T.

   T tiptoed over the rocks to his dresser. He pulled out pajamas.

   Getting ready for bed with no arguments would definitely be helpful. T turned on his radio and did a getting-into-pajamas dance.

"T!" yelled Mama Rex.
"What?" T yelled back, and then remembered. T turned off the radio. He was mostly in his pajamas already, anyway.

T looked around his room. Everything he saw was loud.

He opened his science kit, his puppet theater, and his art box.

"Gluing is a quiet thing to do," yelled T.

"Mmm," said Mama Rex.

SCIENCE KIT!!
BUZZER! ALARM! BELL!

KB EXPRESS

ART

T brought paper and glue to the floor near
Mama Rex.

The glue would not come out of the bottle. T
squeezed. He shook. He poked in a paper clip. He
lay the bottle of glue down on his paper and
punched.

A rainbow of glue spurted out, onto Mama
Rex's sock.

"Oops," whispered T.

T ran to the bathroom and grabbed some toilet paper. Too much toilet paper unrolled.

"Oops," said T.

The toilet paper wouldn't roll up right, so T took the whole huge clump.

T tiptoed back into the living room. He didn't want to interrupt Mama Rex's important project, but he also didn't want to glue his mother to the floor.

T kneeled under the table and bunched up the toilet paper.

"Toilet paper is the quietest type of paper," said T.

"Mmm," answered Mama Rex. She dropped her pencil. "Oops," said Mama Rex.

T picked up the pencil and handed it to Mama Rex.

"Thank you," said Mama Rex.

Under the table, T smiled. T loved being helpful.

T rubbed Mama Rex's sock quietly with the
toilet paper.

"T," said Mama Rex, moving her foot away.

"Well, that's good," answered T. "It can move."

"Shh," whispered Mama Rex.

"Do you like the socks you're wearing?" asked T.

"Hmm?" Mama Rex asked. "Oh, um, yeah.
Mm-hmm. Love 'em."

T tried wiping off the glue again, even quieter.

"Please, T," said Mama Rex. "I really need to concentrate."

"I know," T whispered. He tried wiping more quietly.

The toilet paper was stuck to Mama Rex's sock.

"Oops," said T.

Most of the toilet paper came off in one yank.
T tried to get the extra little bits with his claw.
"T!" yelled Mama Rex. "What are you doing?"
Mama Rex tilted her large head to peer under
the table.
"There's toilet paper glued to the sock you
love," explained T. "I'm quietly ungluing it."
Mama Rex looked down at her sock.
"See?" asked T.
Mama Rex nodded slowly, then sat up.
T couldn't see her face anymore.

"I'm trying to finish this project," said Mama Rex.

"I know," said T. "I'm trying to be helpful."

"Oh," said Mama Rex. "Maybe there's a better way."

T waited under the table, quietly.

"OK, I have an idea," said Mama Rex. "You're a good artist, right?"

"Sort of good, sort of messy," said T.

"We'll put down newspaper," said Mama Rex. "But first, pajamas. No arguing."

T crawled out from under the table and held his arms up.

Mama Rex opened her mouth wide. "What? When? How?"

T smiled. "So what's your idea?" he asked.

Mama Rex took off her gluey sock. "You may stay up past bedtime."

"Hooray!" yelled T.

T loved Mama Rex's ideas, especially when they lasted until after bedtime.

Chapter 3
HELP

T sat in a chair at the table, concentrating. There was newspaper in front of him, and on the newspaper was a folder. T was decorating the folder.

The folder had to be finished in time to carry Mama Rex's work in the morning. Important work deserved a special folder.

T used markers.
He used watercolors.
He used stickers.
He even used stencils, which are very frustrating.

Mama Rex was keeping quiet on her side of the table, working, too.
T turned the folder sideways, then back.
It was good, but something was missing.
T did not know what the something was.

T rummaged through his art box, hoping what-ever was missing was in there. It wasn't.

T glanced up at Mama Rex. She wasn't writing anymore. She was staring out the window.

"Did you finish working?" T asked.

"No," said Mama Rex. She took a deep breath. "I'm thinking."

"Oh," said T.

T turned the folder upside down.

It was good that way, too, but still, something was missing.

T sat back in his chair and stared out the window. He took a deep breath. He took another deep breath. He yawned.

"Getting sleepy?" asked Mama Rex.

"No," said T. "I'm thinking."

Staring out the window wasn't helping T. He decided to stare at the floor instead. The bottle of glue was still lying there, on its side.

"I got it!" yelled T.

T ran to his room and chose his two best rocks. He brought them out into the living room, picked up the glue, and sat in his chair.

Mama Rex was stretching. "Well, I think I'm done," she said.

"Shh," said T. "I really need to concentrate."

T tried his rocks in a few different spots on the folder. When he found the right places, he dribbled some glue there. This time the glue came out perfectly.

T stuck the rocks to the folder. Then he sat back in his chair and looked over his work.

"Want to see?" he asked Mama Rex.

"Yes," said Mama Rex.

T turned the folder so she could get a good view. "You have to let it dry overnight," he explained.

"OK," said Mama Rex. She couldn't take her eyes off the folder T had created. "This is exactly what my work needed."

"Really?" asked T.

"Absolutely," said Mama Rex. "You know which part I like best?"

"Which?" asked T.

"These rocks," Mama Rex said, pointing at them. "I just really like how they're right next to each other."

T smiled. "That's because, see? The bigger one is you, and that one is me."